BY DARRYL MARTEL

Duchess

BY DARRYL MARTEL

DUCHESS

First edition. September 4, 2024.

ISBN: 979-8227590084

Written by Darryl Martel.

Duchess

By

Darryl Martel

Prologue

In the serene countryside of Hertfordshire, amidst the rolling hills and verdant meadows, began the tale of Helen Baxter. Born to humble yet

respectable parents, Helen's early years were marked by simplicity and contentment. Her father, a scholarly gentleman with a love for literature and history, and her mother, a woman of quiet grace and wisdom, instilled in her a sense of integrity and a love for learning.

From a young age, Helen formed a close bond with Elizabeth Bennet, a spirited and intelligent girl from the nearby estate of Longbourn. Their friendship blossomed over shared adventures and heartfelt conversations, each finding in the other a kindred spirit. The two girls, different yet complementary, navigated the trials and joys of youth side by side.

As the years passed, their paths diverged yet remained intertwined.

Elizabeth's journey led her to the grand estate of Pemberley, where she

became the beloved wife of Mr. Fitzwilliam Darcy, a man of great wealth and influence. Helen, ever the faithful friend, often visited Elizabeth, finding solace and joy in their continued companionship.

It was during one of these visits to Pemberley that Helen's destiny took an unexpected turn. There, she met Lord James Percy, the charming and kind-hearted younger son of the Duke and Duchess of Northumberland. Their connection was immediate, a spark that kindled into a deep and abiding love. Despite the differences in their social standing, James saw in Helen the qualities he admired most, sincerity, intelligence, and a compassionate heart.

Their courtship, though not without its challenges, culminated in a proposal that would change Helen's life forever. As she stepped into the world of the Northumberland's, she did so with grace and resilience, supported by the unwavering love of James and the steadfast friendship of Elizabeth.

Helen's journey from the pastoral simplicity of Hertfordshire to the grandeur of Northumberland House was a testament to her strength and character. She faced the scrutiny and expectations of high society with dignity, gradually winning the respect and admiration of those around her. Through trials and triumphs, she remained true to herself, embodying the virtues instilled in her from childhood.

In time, her dedication and compassion endeared her to the Duke and Duchess, and she became a beloved member of their family. Her marriage to James was a union not just of two hearts, but of two worlds, each enriching the other.

As the years went by, Helen's grace and wisdom guided her through the complexities of her new life. When the mantle of the Duchess of Northumberland eventually fell upon her shoulders, she wore it with the same quiet dignity and strength that had always defined her. Her story, a journey from humble beginnings to noble heights, remained a beacon of inspiration to all who knew her.

And so, in the grand halls of Northumberland House, amidst the legacy of history and tradition, Helen Baxter's name was inscribed as one who brought warmth and humanity to the heart of the aristocracy. Her friendship with Elizabeth Darcy, which had begun in the innocence of childhood, endured through the ages, a symbol of the enduring power of love, loyalty, and true companionship.

Returning Home to Longbourn

Elizabeth Darcy, looked out of the carriage window as it rolled through the familiar lanes leading to Longbourn. It had been six, or seven years since she had last visited her childhood home. Now, she was accompanied by her sister Jane, her young children, and her husband, Fitzwilliam Darcy.

Longbourn had changed little in appearance, with its picturesque gardens and cozy manor house standing as a testament to the timelessness of rural England.

The children, William and Thomas, were particularly excited about the visit.

They had heard countless stories from their mother about her childhood

adventures with their aunt Jane, and now they would see the places that had fuelled their imaginations and were always pleased to see their grandparents. Jane, ever the calming presence, sat beside Elizabeth, her serene smile a source of comfort.

As they approached the house, Mr. Bennet stood at the entrance, his eyes crinkling in delight at the sight of his daughters and grandchildren. Mrs. Bennet, as exuberant as ever, bustled out behind him, already calling for the servants to prepare tea and refreshments.

"Elizabeth! Jane! Oh, and the dear little ones!" Mrs. Bennet exclaimed, embracing her daughters and grandchildren with unabashed affection. "Mr. Darcy, welcome, welcome. It is so wonderful to have you all here."

Mr. Bennet chuckled, his eyes twinkling with amusement. "I see your mother has already taken command. Welcome back, my dear girls. And Darcy, always a pleasure."

The family made their way inside, the children eagerly exploring the house under the watchful eyes of their parents. Elizabeth always felt a rush of

nostalgia as she walked through the familiar rooms, each corner filled with memories of her youth.

The following morning, after the initial excitement of their arrival had settled, Elizabeth and Jane were sitting in the parlour with their mother, discussing local news and the changes that had taken place in Meryton since their last visit.

Mrs. Bennet was in the middle of recounting the latest gossip when the butler entered the room, announcing the arrival of a guest.

"Lady Helen Percy has come to call," he declared.

Elizabeth and Jane exchanged surprised glances. Lady Helen, had been a childhood friend, but they had not seen her since one Christmas at Pemberley. The news of her visit was unexpected but welcome. Moments later, Helen entered the room, her face lighting up with a broad smile upon seeing her old friends.

"Helen! What a wonderful surprise!" Jane exclaimed, rising to embrace her.

"It's so good to see you both," Helen replied warmly. "I heard you were visiting, from my aunt's housekeeper and couldn't resist coming over, after visiting my aunt and uncle in Meryton".

"You are welcome here" Mrs Bennett proclaimed.

The friends settled into their chairs, and tea was served. Helen, who had always been lively and full of good humour, looked particularly radiant today. Elizabeth couldn't help but notice a certain sparkle in her eye.

"Tell us, Helen," Elizabeth began, "what has been happening in your life? It's been long since we last saw you."

Helen's smile grew even brighter, and she leaned forward slightly, her voice filled with excitement. "I have the most wonderful news to share, I am with child".

There was a collective gasp from the Bennet women. Even Mr. Darcy, who had entered the room just in time to hear the announcement, looked suitably impressed.

"That's wonderful news!" Mrs. Bennet exclaimed. "My goodness, Helen, that's marvellous news!"

Elizabeth smiled, feeling genuinely happy for her friend. "Tell us more about what it is like being, Lady Helen Percy"

Mr Bennet, who was sipping his tea, jokingly said, "Better than that Lady Catherine de Bourgh, I bet!" He then quickly apologised for saying such a thing, in front of Mr Darcy, who was her nephew.

"Please do not. I believe we all know her Ladyship's character" Darcy said, with a grin looking at Elizabeth.

Helen took a sip of her tea, gathering her thoughts. "The Duke and Duchess of Northumberland are quite grand, as you can imagine. Their estate is enormous, and their presence is very commanding. The Duke is a serious man, but he has a warm heart. The Duchess, well, she reminds me a bit of Lady Catherine!"

Elizabeth raised an eyebrow, intrigued. "Really? In what way?"

"She has a very dignified and imposing manner. She knows her place in society and expects others to respect it. At first, I was quite intimidated by her, but she has a kind side as well. I suppose she just takes some getting used to, but then, she is her ladyship's sister," Helen explained.

"And what about James's brother, Edward, and his wife, Victoria?" Jane asked.

Helen's expression turned thoughtful. "Edward is very much like his father, serious and responsible. Victoria, on the other hand, is quite a character.

She's very elegant and has a strong personality. She, too, reminded me of Lady Catherine. She's very proper and likes things done a certain way. But despite their stern exteriors, they have been welcoming to me."

Elizabeth couldn't help but laugh. "It seems you are fitting into their world quite well, Helen. I'm so happy for you."

"Thank you, Elizabeth," Helen replied. "I'm still getting used to it all, but James has been wonderfully supportive. I'm glad that they have accepted me and I am trying my best".

"How are your parents keeping?" Asked Jane,

"They are in good health and spirits, thank you, they are so proud of me and to marry into such a distinguished family!" Helen replied.

Mr Darcy nodded in agreement. "Indeed. It is a remarkable and fortunate match. But we are sure you are a great asset to the family, Lady Percy".

"Thank you Mr Darcy,"

Elizabeth looked at her husband with a loving smile.

"Your wedding day was wonderful Helen" exclaimed Elizabeth, remembering it with joy.

****

The day of the wedding arrived with clear skies and a gentle breeze. The Percy estate was adorned with flowers and ribbons, transforming it into a scene of breathtaking beauty. Guests from far and wide gathered to witness the union of Miss Helen Baxter and Lord James Percy.

Elizabeth, Jane, and their families were seated among the distinguished guests, marvelling at the splendour of the occasion. The ceremony itself was held in the grand ballroom of the estate, with its high ceilings and crystal chandeliers providing a majestic backdrop.

Helen, dressed in an exquisite gown of ivory satin and lace, walked down the aisle on the arm of her father. She radiated happiness and grace, her eyes never leaving James's as she made her way towards him. The vows were exchanged, and the couple were pronounced husband and wife to the applause of the assembled guests.

The reception that followed was equally grand. Tables were laden with sumptuous food, and a live orchestra provided music for dancing. Elizabeth found herself marvelling at the transformation of her childhood friend into a poised and elegant bride.

As the evening drew to a close, Elizabeth and Darcy took a moment to congratulate the newlyweds.

"Helen, you look absolutely stunning," Elizabeth said, embracing her friend. "We are so happy for you."

"Thank you, Elizabeth," Helen replied, her eyes shining. "I can't believe how perfect everything has been."

Darcy nodded in agreement. "You and Lord Percy make a wonderful couple. We wish you all the happiness in the world."

******

They continued to talk about the day and how admired everyone was, meeting new acquaintances and how happy the day went. Helen also told them about moving into Rosewood House, on the estate and it was a wedding present from the Duke and Duchess. She also spoke of a overseas trip her and Lord Percy were planning, a grand tour of Europe, which was popular at the time. The future sounded so exciting and full of new adventures. Everyone wished them well.

They all spoke about the joy they had shared, not forgetting Lydia and Helen was pleased to hear, who was doing well, after the loss of Mr Wickham. Tea was serviced and as the time came for Helen to depart, she embraced each of them, and Elizabeth, with a smile, said, "Do keep in touch, Helen. Your visits are always a delight." Helen nodded, promising to return soon to Pemberley, her heart warmed by the connection they shared.

****

Six months later, Elizabeth and Darcy were preparing for a visit. This time, they were to host Helen and James at Pemberley, their grand estate in Derbyshire.

The couple had recently returned from a grand tour of Europe, and Elizabeth was eager to hear about their travels.

Pemberley, with its rolling hills and expansive gardens, provided the perfect setting for a reunion. Helen and James arrived in high spirits, regaling their hosts with tales of their adventures in France, Italy, and beyond. Helen looked radiant, blooming with child now.

"It was a wonderful experience," Helen said one evening as they sat by the fire. "We saw so many incredible places and met so many interesting people. But it's good to be back in England and to see you again."

Elizabeth smiled. "We've missed you both. And Pemberley is always more lively with friends around." Elizabeth informed them that, Georgiana was now settled with Colonial Fitzwilliam in Hertfordshire. But came to visit, from time to time.

The days went by and their time at Pemberley was filled with leisurely walks, picnics by the lake, and evenings spent in lively conversation. The bonds of friendship that had been formed in their youth had only grown stronger with time.

One morning, as they were enjoying breakfast, a messenger arrived at Pemberley with urgent news. Elizabeth's heart sank as she saw the expression on Darcy's face as he read the letter.

"Darcy, what is it?" she asked, fearing the worst.

He looked up, his face grave. "It's from Northumberland. There's been a riding accident. Edward is dead, and the Duke and Duchess are gravely injured. James and Helen must return immediately."

Both James and Helen gasped, her hand flying to her mouth. "Oh no! Edward... and the Duke and Duchess... we must go at once."

Darcy nodded. "I'll arrange for a carriage to take you there. We'll make sure you get to Northumberland as quickly as possible."

The mood at Pemberley turned somber as preparations were made for Helen and James's imminent departure. All the house staff helped in the

preparations, the horses prepared. Elizabeth did her best to comfort her friend, but there were no words that could ease the shock and sorrow Helen was feeling.

As they bid farewell to their friends, Elizabeth could only hope that the Duke and Duchess would recover and that Helen and James would find the strength to face the difficult days ahead.

****

<u>A Surprising Turn of Events</u>

A couple of weeks passed before Elizabeth received a letter from Helen. She had been anxiously awaiting news, hoping for some good news about the Duke and Duchess's condition. As she read the letter, her eyes widened in surprise.

"Darcy, you must read this," she said, handing him the letter.

He took it and began to read, his expression mirroring Elizabeth's astonishment.

Dearest Elizabeth,

I hope this letter finds you well. James and I are well. I have so much to tell you that I hardly know where to begin.

The Duke and Duchess are recovering, though it will be a long road to full health . The shock of Edward's death has been felt deeply by all of us. James has been a pillar of strength, and we are doing our best to support his parents through this difficult time.

But there is something else I must tell you, something that has taken us all by surprise. With Edward's death, James has become the heir to the dukedom.

And with the Duke's health in such a fragile state, there have been discussions about the future.

To my utter astonishment, it seems that I am to become the new Duchess of Northumberland. The Duke has expressed his wish for James to take on more responsibilities, and that means I will have to step into a role I never imagined for myself.

I can hardly believe it, Elizabeth. My life has changed so dramatically in such a short time. I only hope I can live up to the expectations and responsibilities that come with this new life as well as becoming a mother, in the not to distant future.

Please give my love to Darcy and the children. I hope we can see each other again soon.

Yours ever, Helen

Darcy looked up from the letter, his expression thoughtful. "This is quite a turn of events. Helen as the Duchess of Northumberland... it's almost unimaginable."

Elizabeth nodded, her mind racing with the implications. "Indeed. But if anyone can rise to the occasion, it's Helen. She has always been strong and resilient. I only hope she finds happiness in her new role."

As they reflected on the changes in their friends' lives, Elizabeth and Darcy felt a renewed appreciation for the stability and happiness they had found together. Life was unpredictable, and they knew that cherishing each moment with loved ones was more important than ever.

******

Helen's transition to her new role as the Duchess of Northumberland would not be without its challenges. The estate was vast, with numerous responsibilities that would require her attention. She had to learn the intricacies of managing a large household, overseeing the staff, and engaging in the social and charitable activities expected of a duchess.

Despite the enormity of the task, Elizabeth knew Helen would approach it with determination and grace. Helen drew upon the lessons she had learned from her mother and from observing the Bennet sisters, and she quickly earned the respect and admiration of those around her.

James, too, would find himself with new responsibilities. As the heir to the dukedom, he had to become more involved in the management of the estate and the family's affairs now. The loss of his brother weighed heavily on him, but he found solace in Helen's unwavering support and their shared commitment to honouring Edward's memory.

Fitzwilliam, turned to Elizabeth, his expression thoughtful and contemplative. "Elizabeth," he began, "I have been reflecting on James's new role as the Duke of Northumberland. Despite the tragic circumstances, I believe he possesses the qualities necessary to be an exemplary Duke. James has always demonstrated a keen sense of responsibility and a profound commitment to his family's legacy. His integrity and fairness are well known, and his dedication to the welfare of those under his care will undoubtedly guide him in this new chapter. Though the weight of the title is heavy, I am confident that James will rise to the occasion with the same honour and dignity that characterised his father." Darcy paused, a hint of a smile touching his lips. "He has Helen by his side, and together, they will navigate these waters with grace and strength."

Elizabeth listened intently to Darcy's reflections, nodding in agreement. "I share your sentiments, Fitzwilliam," she replied thoughtfully. "James has always shown a remarkable balance of wisdom and compassion, qualities that will serve him well as Duke. His genuine concern for others and his ability to lead with empathy are rare virtues. And Helen, with her intelligence and poise, will undoubtedly be his pillar of support. They complement each other beautifully, and together, they embody the strength and grace needed to uphold the family's legacy."

Elizabeth paused, her eyes meeting Darcy's with a look of determination. "In fact, I dare say that James and Helen might make an even better Duke and Duchess than Edward and Victoria. While Edward and Victoria were

undeniably diligent and serious in their duties, James and Helen bring a warmth and approachability that can inspire and unite those around them. Their natural ability to connect with people will endear them to the community and foster a sense of loyalty and respect."

She smiled softly. "Despite the sorrowful circumstances, I believe that James will honour the title with great distinction, and Helen will stand by him as a true Duchess should. They have our unwavering support in this new chapter of their lives."

My Dearest Elizabeth,

I hope this letter finds you in good health and high spirits. I am writing to share the most joyous news with you—our family has been blessed with the arrival of our baby boy, Louis. He entered the world on a bright and beautiful morning, bringing immense happiness and excitement to our household.

Both Louis and I are doing well, and we are already smitten with his charming presence. His arrival has filled our home with such warmth and love, and we are overjoyed to introduce him to you and your wonderful family in the near future.

I am looking forward to the day when we can all gather together and you can meet little Louis. Until then, please convey my warmest regards to Mr. Darcy and give my love to William and Thomas. I eagerly await your next letter and hope to see you soon.

With all my affection, Lady Helen Percy

Elizabeth stood by the window, reading Lady Helen's letter with a smile. As Darcy entered the room, she turned to him, her eyes sparkling with excitement. "Darcy," she said, her voice brimming with joy, "I have the most wonderful news from Lady Helen. She has given birth to a beautiful baby boy named Louis!"

Darcy's face softened with delight as he stepped closer to Elizabeth. "That is splendid news," he replied, taking her hand. "Lady Helen must be

overjoyed."

"Indeed," Elizabeth nodded, "she writes that both she and little Louis are doing well. I can hardly wait to meet him."

"We must send our congratulations immediately," Darcy said, his tone warm. "And perhaps plan a visit soon. It will be lovely to see them and introduce our boys to their new friend."

Elizabeth agreed, already picturing the happy reunion. Together, they began to pen a heartfelt reply, their thoughts filled with anticipation for the joyous meeting to come.

Within weeks a letter arrived at Pemberley.

My Dearest Elizabeth,

I write to you with a heavy heart and profound sadness to share the news of a great loss within our family. The Duke of Northumberland, my dear father-in- law, has succumbed to his injuries and passed away peacefully. His

departure has left us all in deep mourning, and we are enveloped in sorrow at the loss of such a noble and kind-hearted man.

With his passing, my beloved husband has now inherited the title and responsibilities of the Duke of Northumberland. It is with a mixture of solemnity and resolve that we embrace our new roles. Henceforth, I am to be known as the Duchess of Northumberland, a title I shall bear with the utmost respect and dedication.

The Duchess of Northumberland, my husband's mother, now becomes the Dowager Duchess. Her grace and strength during these trying times have

been a source of inspiration to us all. We stand united in our grief, supporting each other through this difficult transition.

I know that you, with your tender heart and understanding nature, will share in our sorrow. Your friendship has always been a source of comfort to me, and I find solace in knowing that you will keep us in your thoughts and prayers during this period of mourning.

Please convey my regards to Mr. Darcy and your family. We look forward to a time when we can meet again under happier circumstances. Until then, we remain steadfast in honouring the legacy of the late Duke and carrying forth the duties bestowed upon us with grace and dignity.

Yours most sincerely, Lady Helen Percy

Duchess of Northumberland

Elizabeth replied later that afternoon.

My Dearest Helen,

We were both deeply moved by your letter and the sorrowful news it

conveyed. Please accept our most heartfelt condolences on the passing of the Duke of Northumberland. Such a significant loss must weigh heavily upon your hearts, and our thoughts and prayers are with you and your family during this time of profound grief.

The Duke was a man of great honour and distinction, and his memory will be cherished by all who had the privilege of knowing him. We can only imagine the depth of the sorrow felt by you, your dear husband, and the Dowager Duchess. We hope that the love and support of your family and friends will provide some comfort and strength as you navigate these difficult days.

It is with a mix of sadness and admiration that we acknowledge your new roles as the Duke and Duchess of Northumberland. We have no doubt that you and Lord Percy will carry out your duties with the same grace and integrity that have always characterised your actions. The legacy of the late Duke will surely be honoured by your dedication and service.

Please know that you are in our hearts and minds here at Pemberley. We join together in extending our deepest sympathies and offers of support. Should there be anything we can do to assist you during this time, please do not hesitate to let us know.

In times of sorrow, the bonds of friendship and family can provide great solace. We hope that the love surrounding you will bring some measure of peace. Though we are separated by distance, please know that our thoughts are with you, and we look forward to the day when we can reunite and offer our support in person.

With all our love and sympathy, Elizabeth and Fitzwilliam Darcy

****

A New Age

Several months later, Helen and James, the new Duke and Duchess of Northumberland invited Elizabeth and Darcy to visit them at the Northumberland estate. They wanted to share their new life and responsibilities with their friends and to seek their counsel on various matters.

Elizabeth and Fitzwilliam Darcy, accompanied by their two sons, William and Thomas, arrived at Northumberland House in their stately carriage, the sound of the horses' hooves echoing against the grand facade. As the carriage came to a halt, a footman stepped forward to open the door, assisting

Elizabeth and the boys as they gracefully descended, with Fitzwilliam following closely. The butler, resplendent in his formal attire, greeted them with a deep bow and escorted the family through the impressive entrance and down the richly adorned corridors. Upon reaching the library, the butler gently knocked before entering, his voice resonating in the hushed, book- lined room as he announced, "Mr. and Mrs. Darcy, with Master William and Master Thomas." James and Helen, the newly titled Duke and Duchess of Northumberland, rose from their seats to welcome their esteemed guests, their faces lighting up at the sight of their dear friends

"Welcome to Northumberland," Helen said, embracing Elizabeth. "I'm so glad you could come."

"It's wonderful to see you, Your Grace," Elizabeth replied. "You've done an incredible job here."

They were warmly greeted by the new Duke and Duchess, Lady Helen Percy, who held baby Louis in her arms. The couple's faces shone with pride and joy as they introduced their son. Elizabeth and Darcy felt an immediate connection with the serene infant, whose presence seemed to embody the promise of a bright future. As they exchanged warm embraces and heartfelt congratulations, the air was filled with the sweetness of familial bonds and the joy of new beginnings.

Over the next few days, Helen and James gave their friends a tour of the estate, sharing stories of their experiences and the challenges they had faced. Elizabeth and Darcy offered their support and advice, drawing on their own experiences of managing Pemberley.

One evening, as they sat in the drawing room, Helen confided in Elizabeth about her hopes and fears for the future.

"Sometimes I wonder if I'm truly capable of fulfilling this role," she admitted. "The responsibilities are immense, and there are so many expectations."

Elizabeth took her friend's hand, offering a reassuring smile. "You are more than capable, Helen. You've always been strong and determined. And you have James by your side. Together, you can overcome any challenge."

Helen nodded, drawing strength from Elizabeth's words. "Thank you, Elizabeth. Your support means the world to me."

****

As the weeks passed and the visit drew to a close, Elizabeth and Darcy reflected on the journey their friends had undertaken. From childhood friends in Meryton to the Duchess of Northumberland, both Helen's and James's

lives had taken a remarkable turn.

Despite the changes and challenges, the bonds of friendship that had been forged in their youth remained as strong as ever. Elizabeth and Darcy knew that no matter where life took them, they would always have each other to rely on.

As they said their goodbyes, Helen and James expressed their gratitude for the support and encouragement they had received from their friends.

"You've been with us through so much," Helen said, her eyes filled with emotion. "We couldn't have done it without you."

Elizabeth embraced her friend, feeling a deep sense of connection and gratitude. "We will always be here for you, Helen. No matter what the future holds, you can count on us." With a final wave, Elizabeth and Darcy departed from Northumberland, carrying with them the memories of their visit and the knowledge that their friendships had only grown stronger with time.

****

The next year or two, were filled with change and growth. Elizabeth and Darcy welcomed their third child, a beautiful baby girl, whom they named Anne, after Darcy's mother. Their home was filled with the laughter and energy of children, and each day brought new joys and challenges.

Helen and Lord Percy's marriage continued to flourish, and they became frequent visitors to Pemberley. Their friendship with the Darcys deepened, and their children grew up together, forming close bonds that would last a lifetime.

The Gardiner's remained an integral part of the Darcy family's life, their visits bringing wisdom and warmth. Jane and Bingley's family grew as well, their home always open to the Darcys and their other loved ones.

Mary and Kitty found their own paths, each finding fulfilment and happiness in their respective endeavours. Mary's music brought joy to many, and Kitty's role as a governess evolved into a loving marriage with a scholarly gentleman who shared her passion for learning.

Lydia's journey, though more complex, also led to a place of peace and contentment. Her friendship with the clergyman's son blossomed into a deep and loving relationship, and they eventually married. Lydia's transformation was a testament to her resilience and the power of love and understanding.

****

Time went on and as the crisp December air settled over the English countryside, Jane and Charles Bingley, now having six children, sent out invitations for a grand Christmas gathering at Netherfield Park. The excitement in the household was palpable as preparations began in earnest. Jane's surprise was immense when the Duke and Duchess of Northumberland graciously accepted their invitation, promising to bring their son and heir, Louis, together with their baby daughter, Isabella, along for the festivities.

The anticipation of such distinguished guests added a layer of thrill and anxiety to the preparations. Netherfield Park was abuzz with activity, as servants and family members alike worked to ensure everything would be

perfect. Elizabeth and Darcy, with their sons William and Thomas with their sister, Victoria Anne, were especially delighted by the prospect of reuniting with their dear friends and introducing their children to one another.

From Kent, Charlotte and Reverend Collins made the journey with their son, David, their presence adding to the sense of a full family reunion. Kitty, Mary, and Lydia, all happily married, arrived with their respective families, Lydia, now married to Robert Cooper, the son of the Reverend Cooper, filling the house with laughter and the merry sounds of children playing.

Mary, married a Clerk who worked for her Uncle Phillips and now very much into her music and Kitty had married, Charles West, the gentleman who employed her as the governess, to his two children, after his wife died.

The Bennett's, now older and cherishing every moment with their expanding family, were particularly pleased to spend such a joyful time with their children and grandchildren. Mr. Bennet's wit and Mrs. Bennet's exuberant pride in her progeny were in full display, making the occasion even more lively.

The highlight of the gathering was undoubtedly the presence of the Duke and Duchess of Northumberland. Their arrival, along with their young son, Louis and baby, Isabella, was met with awe and admiration. The entire household endeavoured to make them feel warmly welcomed, though the grandeur of their titles did little to overshadow the genuine friendships and familial love shared by all.

It was a Christmas to remember, filled with laughter, love, and the creation of cherished memories. Yet, amidst the joy, there was a poignant awareness that time was precious, and for some, this festive season might be their last together. The family held each other a little closer, appreciating the warmth and togetherness that marked this unforgettable Christmas at Netherfield Park.

****

The following year, in July a letter was received at Pemberley.

Dear Fitzwilliam and Elizabeth,

I hope this letter finds you both in good health and high spirits, and that the New Year has brought with it many blessings for you and your family. It is with a heavy heart that I write to you today, bearing news that I know will bring sorrow to you and your loved ones.

It is my solemn duty to inform you of the passing of Lady Catherine de Bourgh. She departed this world peacefully in her sleep on the night of July 12th, at her residence at Rosings Park. The doctors assured us that her end was serene, and she showed no signs of suffering in her final moments.

As you are aware, Lady Catherine was a formidable presence in our lives and in the community. Her strong will and unyielding spirit left an indelible mark on all who knew her. Despite her stern exterior, she had a deep sense of duty to her family and estate, and her absence will be keenly felt by all those at Rosings Park and beyond.

The Dowager Duchess is to saddened and in ill health presently to attend the funeral.

The funeral service is to be held at the parish church in Hunsford, and the interment will take place in the family vault. We have arranged for the service to reflect her stature and her contributions to the community. Given the ties that bind our families, I am certain that your presence would be greatly valued by those in attendance, should you be able to make the journey.

I understand that this news will bring about a period of mourning for you, especially for you, Fitzwilliam, as she was your aunt. The complexities of your relationship notwithstanding, I hope you can find solace in the memories of times past and in the knowledge that she is now at peace.

Please convey my deepest condolences to Georgiana as well. The bond

between family, no matter how strained at times, is a sacred one, and I know that this loss will be felt by her too.

Should you need any assistance in making arrangements for your travels, or any other support during this time, please do not hesitate to reach out. James and I are here for you, and we will do all we can to assist you during this

period of grief.

With deepest sympathies and warmest regards, Helen Percy, Duchess of Northumberland

Elizabeth knew this would upset Darcy, even though they had distanced themselves from Lady Catherine, but always stayed civil with her. Darcy went into his study, informing Elizabeth that he would reply.

Dear Helen,

Thank you for your kind letter dated July 15th, informing us of the passing of my aunt, Lady Catherine de Bourgh. Both Elizabeth and I were deeply

saddened to receive this news, and we extend our heartfelt gratitude for the sensitivity and thoughtfulness with which you conveyed it.

Lady Catherine was indeed a formidable woman whose influence and presence were deeply felt by many. Despite the challenges we sometimes faced in our relationship, I held a deep respect for her dedication to family and her unwavering sense of duty. Her loss is a significant one, and it will be felt keenly by those at Rosings Park and beyond.

Elizabeth and I have shared the news with Georgiana, and she too is deeply affected by our aunt's passing. We are all finding comfort in our shared memories and the support of each other during this time of mourning.

We appreciate your informing us of the arrangements for Lady Catherine's funeral service and interment. It is important to us to honour her memory and pay our respects, and we will make the necessary arrangements to attend the service in Hunsford. Your offer of assistance is very kind, and we may

indeed call upon you if needed.

Your letter reminded us of the strength of the ties that bind our families. We are grateful for your support and the friendship that has grown between our families. Elizabeth and I will carry with us the memories of Lady Catherine, as complex as they may be, and strive to honour her legacy in our own way.

Please convey our deepest sympathies and thanks to James for his support as well. Your presence in our lives is a source of great comfort and strength.

With deepest gratitude and warmest regards,
Fitzwilliam Darcy

Elizabeth thought about her dear friend, Charlotte and wrote a letter to her.

My dear Charlotte,

I hope this letter finds you and Mr. Collins in good health. It is with a heavy heart that I write to you today, having received the sad news of Lady Catherine de Bourgh's passing. Fitzwilliam and I were deeply affected by this news, and I wanted to extend my deepest sympathies to both you and Mr. Collins during this difficult time.

I can only imagine the profound sense of loss Mr. Collins must be

experiencing. His respect and admiration for Lady Catherine were well known, and I know her passing will be a significant blow to him. Please

convey to him our heartfelt condolences and assure him that our thoughts are with him.

Fitzwilliam and I plan to attend the funeral service at Hunsford. It is important to us to pay our respects to Lady Catherine and to offer our support to you and Mr. Collins. While the occasion is a somber one, it will be good to see you again, dear friend, and to offer what comfort we can.

I am also writing to inquire about Miss Anne de Bourgh. Given Lady Catherine's passing, I am concerned about her future. Will she continue to reside at Rosings Park? I imagine this transition must be particularly challenging for her, and I wonder what her plans might be.

Please write back at your earliest convenience, Charlotte, and let me know how you and Mr. Collins are faring. If there is anything we can do to assist you during this time, do not hesitate to let us know. We look forward to seeing you soon, despite the unfortunate circumstances.

With deepest sympathy and warm regards, Elizabeth Darcy

****

My dear Elizabeth,

Thank you for your kind and thoughtful letter. Your words of sympathy and support have brought much comfort to Mr. Collins and myself during this sorrowful time. Lady Catherine's passing has indeed been a great shock, and Mr. Collins is deeply saddened by the loss of his esteemed patroness.

We are heartened to hear that you and Mr. Darcy will be attending the funeral. It will be a great comfort to see familiar and supportive faces. Your presence will undoubtedly be a source of strength for us both.

Regarding your inquiry about Miss Anne de Bourgh, there have been surprising developments. Contrary to what many might have expected, Anne has expressed a desire to leave Rosings Park. She has long felt stifled by the strictures placed upon her by Lady Catherine, and with her mother's passing, she sees an opportunity to seek a life of her own choosing. She has decided to visit relatives in Bath and consider her options for the future. It is a bold move for her, and I am cautiously optimistic that this will lead to a more fulfilling and independent life for Anne.

We appreciate your concern and your readiness to assist. The support of dear friends like you and Mr. Darcy means the world to us in these trying times. I look forward to seeing you both at the funeral and catching up, even if under such sad circumstances.

With warmest regards and deepest thanks, Charlotte Collins

****

The day of Lady Catherine de Bourgh's funeral dawned grey and somber, reflecting the mood of those gathered to pay their respects. As Fitzwilliam and Elizabeth Darcy approached the parish church of Hunsford, the scene before them was one of solemn grandeur. A black horse-drawn hearse, adorned with elegant black plumes, stood at the ready, its presence commanding the attention of all who passed. The horses, draped in black, waited patiently, their silent dignity adding to the gravity of the occasion.

Crowds of people, both villagers and those who had traveled from afar, filled the churchyard and spilled onto the surrounding grounds. Lady Catherine had been a prominent figure, and it seemed that everyone, whether out of respect, duty, or curiosity, had come to witness her final journey.

As the Darcys made their way through the gathered throng, nods and murmured greetings acknowledged their presence. Elizabeth felt a pang of sympathy for Anne de Bourgh, who stood stoically by the hearse, receiving condolences with quiet grace. Despite the reserved nature of their relationship, Anne had lost her mother, and the pain of that loss was etched clearly on her face.

Inside the church, the atmosphere was thick with reverence. The interior, draped in black, was filled to capacity. Elizabeth and Darcy found their seats near the front, alongside Georgiana, Colonel Fitzwilliam, and the Duke and Duchess of Northumberland. The service began with the mournful strains of the organ, filling the space with a somber melody that set the tone for the

proceedings.

The opening hymn, "Abide with Me," was sung with heartfelt emotion by the congregation, the words a poignant reminder of the fleeting nature of life. The minister spoke eloquently of Lady Catherine's contributions to the community, her strength of character, and her unyielding dedication to Rosings Park and its legacy. Despite the complexities of their relationship, Elizabeth found herself reflecting on Lady Catherine's impact and the ways in which she had shaped the lives of those around her.

Following the eulogy, another hymn, "The Lord is My Shepherd," filled the church, the familiar words providing comfort to many. Elizabeth glanced at Fitzwilliam, whose expression was one of quiet contemplation. She squeezed his hand gently, offering her silent support.

The congregation followed the coffin out of the church and proceeded to the family vault, where Lady Catherine would be laid to rest. The hearse led the way, its slow, measured pace matched by the mourners who walked behind. The black plumes of the horses bobbed gently with each step, a silent accompaniment to the sound of shuffling feet and hushed whispers.

At the graveside, the minister's words were brief but poignant, commending Lady Catherine's soul to the care of the Almighty. As the coffin was lowered into the vault, a final hymn, "Amazing Grace," was sung. The haunting melody and its message of redemption and hope echoed through the churchyard, a fitting farewell to a woman of such formidable presence.

The congregation made their way back to Rosings Park, where the house seemed unusually quiet, the weight of recent events hanging heavy in the air. The Duke and Duchess of Northumberland, along with Georgiana and Colonel Fitzwilliam, their presence a comforting reminder of the bonds of family and friendship.

Over the next few days, Rosings became a place of quiet reflection and mutual support. Conversations were held in hushed tones, and the shared grief brought the occupants closer together. Elizabeth spent time with Anne, offering her a listening ear and gentle companionship. Anne, in turn, expressed her gratitude for the support and began to open up about her plans for the future.

"I have decided to spend some time in Bath," Anne confided to Elizabeth one afternoon. "I need a change of scenery and the opportunity to forge a new path for myself. Rosings has been my entire world for so long, and I feel it is time to see what else life has to offer."

Elizabeth nodded, understanding the courage it took for Anne to make such a decision. "I think that is a wonderful idea, Anne. A change of scenery can do wonders for the soul, and you deserve the chance to explore new

possibilities."

As the days passed, the atmosphere at Rosings began to lighten. The presence of friends and family brought a sense of normalcy and hope for the future.

Elizabeth and Fitzwilliam found solace in the company of those they loved, and the bonds that had been strengthened by shared sorrow provided a foundation for healing.

When it was time for the Darcys to return to Pemberley, they left Rosings with a renewed sense of purpose and gratitude for the support of their family and friends. Lady Catherine's passing had marked the end of an era, but it had also paved the way for new beginnings and the possibility of growth and change.

As they made their way home, Elizabeth looked forward to the future with a sense of optimism. Life, with all its challenges and uncertainties, was made more bearable by the love and support of those around her. Together, they would honour the past while embracing the promise of what lay ahead.

One afternoon, as the sun cast a warm, golden light over the drawing-room at Rosings Park, Elizabeth and Darcy found themselves enjoying a quiet moment of respite over afternoon tea. The atmosphere was one of calm and camaraderie, a welcome break from the somber mood that had pervaded the house since Lady Catherine's passing. Georgiana was playing a soft melody on the pianoforte, and the Duke and Duchess of Northumberland were seated nearby, engaged in light conversation.

Helen, the Duchess of Northumberland, looked thoughtful as she sipped her tea. She glanced at Elizabeth and Darcy, her expression one of curiosity mixed with genuine interest. "Fitzwilliam, Elizabeth, there is something I have been meaning to discuss with you both. I hope you don't mind my bringing it up."

Darcy set his teacup down and looked at Helen with a reassuring smile. "Of course, Helen. Please, feel free to speak your mind."

Helen took a moment to gather her thoughts before continuing. "During the

past few days, as we have all been reflecting on Lady Catherine's life and the connections between our families, I came across some fascinating information about our shared lineage. I was not aware until recently that your mother, Anne, Lady Catherine, and my mother-in-law, the Dowager Duchess, were sisters."

Elizabeth's eyes widened in surprise, and she looked at Darcy, who seemed equally taken aback. "I did not realise our families were so closely connected," Elizabeth remarked. "It is quite a revelation."

Helen nodded. "Indeed, it is. The three sisters were daughters of an Earl, and from what I have learned, they were all set to marry very well. Fitzwilliam, I was curious if you knew much about your mother's childhood and her relationship with her sisters."

Darcy leaned back in his chair, his expression thoughtful. "I know a few things about my mother's childhood. She spoke fondly of her time growing up with her sisters. They were close, though their lives took them in different directions as they married and started their own families. My mother, Anne, married my father, and they were deeply devoted to each other. She often spoke of Lady Catherine with a mixture of admiration and exasperation, and she held a great deal of respect for their sister, your mother-in-law the

Dowager Duchess."

Helen smiled warmly. "It is heartening to hear that they maintained such strong bonds despite the distances that life placed between them. From what I have gathered, the three sisters were quite remarkable in their own ways. Lady Catherine, with her formidable presence and dedication to Rosings; your mother, Anne, who was known for her grace and kindness; and my mother-in-law who has always been a pillar of strength and wisdom."

Elizabeth listened intently, her curiosity piqued. "What more can you tell us about their early lives, Helen?"

Helen set her teacup down and leaned forward slightly, her voice taking on a more animated tone. "Well, the sisters were raised at their father's estate, a grand and beautiful place. They were given the finest education and were well-versed in the arts and literature. Their father, the Earl, was a man of great influence, and he ensured that his daughters were prepared for their roles in society. The sisters were often the centre of attention at social gatherings, admired for their beauty and intelligence."

Darcy nodded, a faint smile playing on his lips. "I remember my mother telling me about the grand balls and gatherings at their father's estate. She spoke of them with a certain nostalgia, though she always emphasised the importance of humility and kindness."

Helen continued, "As they grew older, each sister made her mark in her own way. Lady Catherine's strong will and determination led her to Sir Lewis de Bourgh and to manage Rosings with an iron hand. Your mother, Lady Anne, brought warmth and compassion to Pemberley, by marrying your father, David Darcy. And my mother-in-law, the Dowager Duchess, has been a guiding light for our family, always offering sage advice and support."

Elizabeth glanced at Darcy, who seemed deeply moved by Helen's words. "It is clear that they were extraordinary women," Elizabeth said softly. "Their legacy lives on in their children and grandchildren."

Helen nodded. "Indeed, it does. I feel a deep sense of pride and connection knowing that we are all part of that legacy. And it is comforting to know that despite the years and the distances, the bonds of family remain strong."

As the afternoon light began to fade, the conversation continued, weaving together stories of the past with hopes for the future. In that moment, surrounded by family and friends, Elizabeth and Darcy felt a profound sense of belonging and a renewed appreciation for the ties that bound them to those who had come before.

The days spent at Rosings Park, reflecting on their shared history and supporting one another, had strengthened the bonds between them all. As they prepared to return to their own lives, they carried with them a deeper

understanding of their heritage and a commitment to honouring the legacy of the remarkable women who had shaped their families.

****

The tranquil gardens of Rosings Park provided a serene backdrop for a rare moment of privacy between Elizabeth and Charlotte. The two friends walked side by side, their steps leisurely as they enjoyed the peace and beauty of the well-tended grounds. The air was crisp, and the early spring flowers were

beginning to bloom, adding splashes of colour to the landscape.

Elizabeth glanced at Charlotte, noting the contemplative expression on her friend's face. "It is lovely to have this time to ourselves, Charlotte. It feels like ages since we've had a proper conversation."

Charlotte smiled, though there was a hint of nervousness in her eyes. "Yes, it is wonderful to catch up, Elizabeth. There is something I have been meaning to tell you, something that has weighed heavily on my heart for a long time."

Elizabeth's curiosity was piqued. "You know you can tell me anything, Charlotte. What is it that troubles you?"

They walked in silence for a few moments, the sound of their footsteps mingling with the distant chirping of birds. Finally, Charlotte took a deep breath and spoke in a hushed tone. "Elizabeth, there is a secret I have kept for many years, a secret that involves my son, David. I have carried this burden alone, and I feel I must share it with someone I trust."

Elizabeth's concern deepened. "Charlotte, you can trust me. What is it?"

Charlotte hesitated, then continued, her voice barely above a whisper. "David is not Mr. Collins's son. His father is... was... a gardener here at Rosings Park. A mature, handsome man named Robert."

Elizabeth's eyes widened in surprise, but she quickly composed herself. "Charlotte, I had no idea. How did this happen?"

Charlotte looked away, her expression one of deep regret. "It happened years ago, shortly after we were married. Mr. Collins was often preoccupied with his duties, and I found myself spending more time in the gardens. Robert was kind, attentive, and we formed a bond. It was wrong, I know, but it happened, and David was the result of that liaison."

Elizabeth smiled, they both looked at each other with a knowing look and both quietly laughed.

Elizabeth placed a comforting hand on Charlotte's arm. "Thank you for trusting me with this, Charlotte. It must have been incredibly difficult for you to keep this secret for so long. Does Mr. Collins know?"

Charlotte shook her head. "No, he does not. And for David's sake, it must remain that way. Mr. Collins has always believed David to be his own, and I cannot bear the thought of the truth destroying our family."

Elizabeth nodded, her expression resolute. "Your secret is safe with me, Charlotte. I promise I will never speak of this to anyone."

Charlotte's eyes filled with gratitude. "Thank you, Elizabeth. Your friendship means more to me than I can say. I have carried this secret for so long, and sharing it with you has lightened my burden."

They walked in silence for a while longer, the bond between them strengthened by this shared confidence. Elizabeth knew that Charlotte had made a difficult choice, one that had weighed heavily on her heart for years. As they continued their walk through the gardens, Elizabeth vowed to support her friend in any way she could.

The sun began to set, casting a golden glow over the landscape. The two friends made their way back to the house, their steps lighter and their hearts a little less burdened. The secret they now shared would remain between them, a testament to the strength of their friendship and the trust they placed in each other.

As they approached the house, Elizabeth squeezed Charlotte's hand reassuringly. "We will face whatever comes together, Charlotte. You are not alone."

Charlotte smiled, her eyes shining with a mixture of relief and gratitude. "Thank you, Elizabeth. Your support means everything to me."

With that, they rejoined the others, their secret safe and their friendship stronger than ever.

****

As they prepared to leave Rosings, Miss Anne de Bourgh approached

Elizabeth and Darcy with a thoughtful expression. "I wanted to thank you both for being here during this difficult time. Your support has meant more to me than I can express. And Helen, your revelations about our family's history have given me a renewed sense of pride and purpose."

Darcy placed a reassuring hand on Anne's shoulder. "We are family, Anne. We will always be here for you."

Elizabeth smiled warmly. "Yes, Anne. And remember, you are not alone. We are all here to support you as you move forward."

Anne nodded, her eyes shining with gratitude. "Thank you. I will carry your words with me as I embark on this new chapter of my life."

With their farewells exchanged and promises to stay in close contact,

Elizabeth and Darcy left Rosings Park, their hearts full of hope and a renewed sense of connection to their family's storied past. The journey ahead was uncertain, but they knew that with the strength of their family and the love they shared, they could face whatever the future held.

****

Elizabeth and Darcy returned to Pemberley, their hearts filled with gratitude for the stability and happiness they had found together. They watched their children grow, cherishing each moment and drawing strength from the love they shared

Sadly the Dowager Duchess passed away some months after, but she took comfort in the knowledge that the estate was in good hands. The new Duke and Duchess of Northumberland were loved and respected by everyone, their compassion, empathy and sympathy, vision of a bright future, they looked after their tenants and servants equally and made a great inheritance for Louis, who would one day, be the next Duke of Northumberland.

As the years passed, the bonds between the families remained unbroken. They celebrated each other's joys and supported each other through life's challenges, knowing that true friendship was a treasure beyond measure.

Helen and James's story was a testament to the power of resilience and the strength of the human spirit. Through loss and hardship, they had found a new beginning, embracing their roles with courage and grace. And in doing so, they had created a legacy of love and friendship that would endure for generations to come.

Years later, as Elizabeth and Darcy sat together on the terrace at Pemberley, watching their grandchildren play in the gardens, they reflected on the journey that had brought them to this moment.

"Life has a way of surprising us, doesn't it?" Elizabeth mused, her eyes twinkling with the wisdom of years.

Darcy nodded, his hand gently clasping hers. "Indeed it does. But through all the twists and turns, one thing has remained constant."

"And what's that?" Elizabeth asked, a smile playing on her lips.

"The love and friendship we've shared," Darcy replied. "It's the foundation of everything."

Elizabeth leaned her head against his shoulder, feeling a deep sense of contentment. "Yes, it is. And it's a legacy worth cherishing."

As they watched the next generation explore the beauty of Pemberley, Elizabeth and Darcy knew that the bonds they had forged with Helen and

James, and the love they had nurtured within their own family, would continue to shape the future in ways they could only imagine.

And so, with hearts full of gratitude and hope, they embraced the journey ahead, knowing that the legacy of love and friendship they had created would endure for all time.

The End

About the Author

Darryl Martel - Delve into a realm where imagination knows no bounds, where the ethereal dance of words paints vivid tapestries of the mind.

Through the nimble strokes of storytelling, I navigate realms both real and fantastical, crafting narratives that whisper secrets of the human condition. Each word is a brushstroke, each sentence a melody, weaving together a tapestry of emotion, intrigue, and revelation.

* 9 7 9 8 2 2 7 5 9 0 0 8 4 *